The magic took them to
a castle.

1

Three witches lived in the castle.
They were nasty witches.

One was a black witch.
One was a red witch.
One was a green witch.

The magic took the children inside
the castle.
It took them to a room.

A frog was in the room.
'I am a king,' said the frog.
'I am the king of this castle.'

'The witches turned me into a frog.
Help me,' he said.

A witch was coming.
It was the black witch.
'Look out!' said the frog.

The witch opened the door.
Gran pushed the witch.
Chip took the witch's keys.

They ran out of the room.
Chip locked the door.
The witch couldn't get out.

Everyone ran.
'Look out!' called Chip.

A witch was coming.
It was the red witch.

'I don't like witches,' said Gran.
She put a net over the witch.

The witch couldn't get out.
'Good old Gran,' called Biff.

Gran went to the green witch.
'I don't like witches,' said Gran.
'I don't like nasty witches.'

Gran threw the witch on the floor.
'Help!' yelled the witch.
'Good old Gran,' said the children.

Some frogs came in and
    jumped on the table.
One was the king.

'Help us,' he said.
Biff and Gran looked in
the witches' book.

The frogs turned into people.
'Thanks!' said the king.

The witches turned into frogs.
Gran put the book on the fire.
'Oh no!' said the witches.

The king had a party.
Everyone went to it.
'What a good party!' said Chip.

'What an adventure!' said Biff.
'I like adventures,' said Gran.
'Good old Gran!' said everyone.

The magic key was glowing.
'It's time to go,' said Biff.
'Goodbye,' said the king.

The magic took them back to
Biff's room.

They fell on to Biff's bed.
'Oh no!' said Mum.